THE MONKEY KING
Makes Fire on Black Wind Mountain

Based on *Journey to the West*
by Wu Cheng'en

New Translation by Li Chaoyuan

Illustrations by Liu Jikun

WFP
WORDFIRE PRESS

朝華出版社
BLOSSOM PRESS

EBook ISBN: 978-1-68057-485-2
Trade Paperback ISBN: 978-1-68057-486-9
Hardcover ISBN: 978-1-68057-487-6

Cover design by Janet McDonald
Adapted by Firethorn
Review by Scott Huntsman
Edited and Adapted by Rebecca Moesta
Published by
WordFire Press, LLC
PO Box 1840
Monument CO 80132

Kevin J. Anderson & Rebecca Moesta, Publishers
WordFire Press eBook Edition 2022
WordFire Press Trade Paperback Edition 2022
WordFire Press Hardcover Edition 2022
Printed in the USA

Join our WordFire Press Readers Group for
sneak previews, updates, new projects, and giveaways.

Sign up at wordfirepress.com

Review

Previously, the Jade Emperor asked the Buddha to help subdue the Monkey King (Sun Wukong), who had wreaked havoc in Heaven. The Buddha created the Mountain of Five Elements and imprisoned the Monkey King beneath it.

Five centuries later, Emperor Taizong of the Tang Dynasty sent a respected Buddhist monk, Master Xuanzang, on a quest to get Buddhist scriptures from the Western Continent. On his way west, the monk rescued Wukong.

Enlightened by the Bodhisattva Guanyin, the Monkey King converted to Buddhism, became the disciple of Master Xuanzang, and pledged to guard the monk all the way to the Western Continent.

Because she knew Wukong was still unruly, Guanyin gave the monk a cap with a golden band to put on the Monkey King's head. She taught the monk a band-tightening spell to punish Wukong with a headache if he disobeyed. After a few terrible headaches, Wukong promised to behave.

Guanyin also transformed a small dragon into a white dragon horse to carry Master Xuanzang on his journey.

After being imprisoned under the Mountain of Five Elements for over 500 years, the Monkey King was finally rescued by the monk Xuanzang. Wukong also converted to Buddhism, became Master Xuanzang's disciple, and offered to protect him on his journey to the west.

One evening, they came upon a Guanyin monastery and asked for lodging.

Xuanzang and his disciple arrived at the monastery, where an old monk assisted by two young monks welcomed them.

The old monk said, "I am Elder Jinchi, abbot of this monastery. My disciples told me that a master from Tang had arrived, so I came to greet you."

Xuanzang thanked him and asked about his age out of respect.

"I am two hundred seventy years old," Jinchi said.

As they talked, a young monk served three cups of fragrant tea in gold-rimmed cups. Xuanzang admired them. "Marvelous. How exquisite these cups are!"

Abbot Jinchi said, "It is nothing. You are from the prosperous Tang and must have seen countless treasures. I wonder if you have any such magnificent valuables to show me."

When Xuanzang humbly declined, the Monkey King blurted out, "But Master, don't you have a precious robe in your bag?"

Jinchi smiled. "I have been a monk here for more than 250 years, and I own seven or eight hundred robes." The abbot then asked his assistant to bring his robes, which were all beautifully embroidered with gold.

Wukong chuckled. "Put those away! Put them away! Let me show you ours."

Master Xuanzang whispered, "Disciple, do not show off our wealth. As the ancient saying goes, hide your treasures from greedy and cunning eyes, lest you invite disaster."

Wukong, however, would not listen. "Don't worry so much. I know what I am doing." He rushed to the bag. The moment he opened it, a bright glow burst forth. As soon as he removed the wrapping, took out the robe, and displayed it, the room flooded with waves of colorful light in every hue of the rainbow.

All of the monks were amazed.

The precious robe kindled a flame of envy in Abbot Jinchi. He knelt in front of Xuanzang and begged, "It is getting late, and my eyes are too dim to admire this treasure. Would you please let me have it for one night so I can take a closer look?"

Xuanzang was taken aback by his request and blamed Wukong for creating the problem.

Wukong smirked and said, "Why are you so afraid of him?" Despite Master Xuanzang's reluctance, the Monkey King handed the robe to Jinchi.

Once he had the robe in his hands, Jinchi took it to a back room to admire it under the lamp. The abbot wanted the luxurious robe so badly that he despised himself for not being able to keep it, and he burst into tears.

A young monk said, "What is so difficult? Why don't we set a fire outside the room where they are sleeping? Once they burn to death, won't the robe be ours?"

Because the other monks also coveted the robe, they all agreed to the plan.

Xuanzang and the Monkey King had already gone to sleep in the guest room. As a divine monkey, though, Wukong was vigilant even in his sleep. He heard people walking around and the rustling of firewood. *Why would there be so many footsteps in the middle of the night? he wondered. Could thieves be coming to kill us?"* He sprang off bed, transformed himself into a bee, and went to see what was going on.

He saw monks placing firewood and dry grass around their room, preparing to set fire to it.

The Monkey King gave a secret smile. *Master was right! That monk does want to kill us and steal our robe. He is frail, so if I hit him with my iron staff, I am likely to beat him up. And if he dies, Master will blame me for murder. No, no, no! Forget it! Just let them carry out their plan and I will deal with the fire.*

The Monkey King mounted a cloud, somersaulted to Heaven's South Gate, went in, and found the Western Heavenly King.

"My master is in great danger from men trying to set him on fire," Wukong said. "May I borrow your fireproof cloak to save him? Please—it is urgent."

Knowing the temper and powers of the Monkey King, the Western Heavenly King immediately gave him the protective cloak.

The Monkey King covered Xuanzang, the dragon horse, and their bags with the cloak. Wukong himself sat on rooftop above the abbot's room to protect the robe.

Once the fire took hold, Wukong breathed out a gust of wind to spread the fire until the entire monastery was engulfed in red flames.

Chaos broke out. Monks shouted and fled the burning building, carrying boxes and cages and tables and pots out into the courtyard.

Twenty miles south of the monastery, was Black Wind Mountain. In a cave in that mountain, a Black Wind Monster made his home. When he awoke from his dreams, he noticed that fire shone brightly from the north. He hurried outside and headed north. He sent clouds to douse the fire, but smoke and flames had spread everywhere except the back room, and on the rooftop sat a watchman.

The monster rushed inside to put out the fire, only to see a colorful glow in Abbot Jinchi's room coming from a bag on the table. He opened the bag, discovered the precious robe, and was filled with greed. Taking advantage of the fire, he stole the robe and took it to his cave.

The big fire did not stop until dawn.

The Monkey King returned the fireproof cloak to the Western Heavenly King.

When Xuanzang woke up, he was astonished to find everything burned to the ground.

"Master, that old abbot was so envious of our robe that he set a fire to burn us." Wu-kong chuckled. "But I protected our room and 'helped' their fire along with a gust of wind."

Xuanzang was shocked,. "How on earth was that helping? You should have put it out with water!"

"I would not have brought wind if he had not made a fire," Wukong said.

Xuanzang asked anxiously, "Where is the robe? It did not burn, did it?"

"Relax, Master. It is intact," said the Monkey King. "I made sure that the room where the abbot put your robe never caught fire. Wait while I fetch it, and we can get back to our journey."

Abbot Jinchi was agitated because he could not find the precious robe anywhere, and the whole monastery was destroyed. Then he heard that Xuanzang was still alive and wanted his robe back. The abbot became so anxious that he ran straight into a pillar, hit his head hard, and died.

The Monkey King summoned all of the monks, searched them one by one, and looked through every chest that survived the fire. The robe was nowhere to be found.

Furious with Wukong, Xuanzang recited the band-tightening spell.

Monkey fell to the ground clutching his head and screaming, "Stop, Master! Stop! I swear I'll find your robe."

Seeing Wukong so miserable, the monks all knelt to beg for mercy on his behalf. Only then did Master Xuanzang finally stop reciting the spell.

The Monkey King searched every inch of the monastery, but there was still no sign of the robe. He pondered for a while and asked, "Do any monsters live nearby?"

"Black Wind Mountain is twenty miles south of here. In that mountain is Black Wind Cave, where the Black Wind Monster lives," replied a monk.

"Then that monster must have stolen the robe. I am going to track him down," Wu-kong said. He asked the monks to take good care of Xuanzang and the horse, and then launched a somersault to Black Wind Mountain.

Amazed and frightened by the Monkey King's powers, the monks bowed to him.

The Monkey King soon saw three people sitting on a grassy slope of the mountain and talking loudly: a tanned man, a Taoist priest, and a scholar dressed in white. The tanned man said, "I found an amazing treasure last night, a shining embroidered Buddhist robe. The day after tomorrow on my birthday, I will invite all Taoists from the mountains to come and admire the treasure. Maybe I will call the party the 'Robe Banquet.'"

The Monkey King was enraged. He jumped off of the cloud with his Obedient Gold-Banded Staff lifted high and shouted, "How dare you have a banquet to show off a robe stolen from me! Give it back to me now!" The Monkey King hit them with his iron staff, but the tanned man turned into a gust of wind and fled, the Taoist escaped on a cloud, and only the scholar was killed. When the Monkey King bent to check the body, he found nothing but a white snake, since the scholar was actually a snake demon.

The Monkey King went to search for the tanned man. He finally found a cave with two closed stone gates. A horizontal stone slab over the door said

BLACK WIND CAVE

The Monkey King immediately swung his iron staff and shouted, "Open the door!"

A small guard imp opened the door and asked, "Who are you that you dare to assault our divine cave?"

"What kind of place is this that you dare to call it divine? You don't deserve to use that word." Wukong chided. "Go quickly and tell your king to send my master's robe back, and I will spare your lives!"

The imp rushed inside to report.

The Black Wind Monster had just gotten home after being attacked by the strange monkey. When the Black Wind Monster heard the message, he thought, *Who is this rude fellow, who arrives from nowhere and then comes to my home to shout at me?* He put on his cloak, grabbed a tasseled spear, and walked out of the cave.

The monster roared, "What kind of monk are you that you presume to speak to me? That was reckless!"

Wukong jumped in front of him shaking his staff and shouted, "Stop your blustering! Give me the old master's robe immediately!"

The monster said, "Where are you from, monk? How should I know where you lost your robe? Why are you coming to me to ask for it?"

"My robe was stored in the abbot's room of the monastery," Wukong said. "You stole it during the fire and even wanted to show it off at your birthday party. Don't deny it! Now give it back to me and I will spare your life. Otherwise I will tear down all of Black Wind Mountain and turn your cave to rubble."

"Where are you from? What is your family name? How powerful are you that you take the risk of boasting in front of me?" sneered the Black Wind Monster.

"I am the Monkey King, Sun Wukong, now the disciple of Master Xuanzang from Tang. Travel the world and ask around. Everyone knows my reputation," Wukong said.

The Black Wind Monster smirked. "So you are the stable boy who made trouble in Heaven."

The Monkey King hated to be called a stable boy. He was outraged. "You vile monster! You stole the robe and offended my master! Stay there and meet my iron staff!"

The monster dodged and swung his spear to fight. They went back and forth for a dozen rounds but neither could win.

They fought till noon and the monster said, "I call a truce! After I eat my lunch, we will fight again."

"Don't leave! Give back the robe first and then eat!" the Monkey King said.

The monster made a feint, went back into the cave, and closed the stone door. He called back his imps to plan the upcoming banquet and send invitations to demon kings on other mountains.

Unable to get into the cave, the Monkey King went back to the monastery for the time being.

Xuanzang asked, "Wukong, did you find the robe?"

"Yes, it was stolen by a monster on Black Wind Mountain," said the Monkey King.

All the monks were relieved to hear that at least Wukong knew where the robe was.

"Don't get too excited yet! I haven't brought the robe back. Only when I bring it back and my master leaves the monastery in good health, should you feel at peace. Otherwise you will provoke me," the Monkey King warned.

"They are taking good care of me," Master Xuanzang assured him. "Just go and get the robe back."

The Monkey King rode a cloud back to Black Wind Mountain. On his way, he spotted an imp walking down the main road with a rosewood box under his arm. Wukong thought that invitations must be inside the box, so he swung his iron staff and killed the little monster.

The Monkey King picked up the box and found that it held an invitation for the old monk Jinchi.

Wukong burst into laughter. *That sly old abbot was conspiring with the monster all along! That could explain why he lived so long. I still remember his appearance. If I look like him, maybe I can get into the cave to take the robe back.*

The Monkey King recited a spell into the wind and transformed himself to look exactly like Abbot Jinchi. He went to the cave entrance and called, "Open the door!"

An imp opened the door and recognized Jinchi. He hurried and reported to the monster, "Your Majesty, Elder Jinchi is here."

The monster was surprised. "Oh? Why did he come so quickly? I've only just sent a messenger to deliver the invitation. He couldn't have gotten here so soon. Perhaps Master Xuanzang convinced him to come and ask for the robe." The Black Wind Monster immediately ordered his imp to hide the robe and not let anyone see it.

When the Monkey King entered the cave, the Black Wind Monster greeted him, wearing a black and green robe and a pair of suede boots.

Wukong said, "I was on my way to visit you and ran into your messenger with the invitation. I heard about the Robe Banquet, so I hurried here to see you."

"That is strange. The robe belonged to the Tang monk who stays in your monastery. Do not tell me you have not seen it there. Why bother coming here to see it?" asked the monster with a smile.

"I did borrow it from the Tang monk, but you took it before I had the chance to open the bag, so I came here to admire it," Wukong said.

While they were talking, a patrol imp reported in. "Your Majesty, my brother who was carrying the invitation was killed on the road by the Monkey King. The Monkey King then turned into Elder Jinchi to trick us and steal the robe."

The Black Wind Monster picked up his spear and stabbed at Wukong. Meanwhile, the Monkey King took his gold-banded iron staff from his ear, changed it to the proper size, and fought the monster with it.

They fought from the cave to the mountain, and from the mountain to the clouds. The air was full of fog and wind and blowing sand. It was a long and hard fight that lasted till dark, but they were at a stalemate.

"It is getting late. Why don't we wait until tomorrow morning to settle everything?" suggested the monster.

Wukong ignored him and continued fighting.

As before, the monster turned into a gust of wind and went back to his cave.

Again the Monkey King returned to the monastery.

Seeing that he did not have the robe, Master Xuanzang asked, "What happened this time?"

"We had a long fight, and it was a tie," Wukong explained.

"Then how do you plan to defeat him and get the robe back?" the master asked.

The Monkey King smiled. "I have a plan."

The next morning, Wukong jumped up and got ready to leave.

Xuanzang stopped him and asked, "Where are you going?"

"To find Guanyin. This monastery was built in her honor. I will go and ask her to help us by personally telling the monster to return the robe," said the Monkey King.

In the blink of an eye, the Monkey King traveled to Guanyin's place in the South Sea.

A deity came out to greet him and asked, "Shouldn't you be protecting a Tang monk on his travels west?"

Wukong said, "There is something I need that will help protect my master. Would you please tell Guanyin I am here?"

After the deity announced his arrival, the Monkey King met with Guanyin and told her the whole story.

Guanyin said, "This happened because you showed off your treasure and brought it to the attention of greedy people. Your wind also fanned the fire that burned my monastery. How dare you ask for my help?"

Wunkong bowed humbly. "Please forgive me, Bodhisattva. Have mercy, and please help me catch that monster."

Guanyin said, "That monster has many powers, just as you do. Well, for your master's sake, I will go with you."

They headed for Black Wind Mountain on a cloud.

They landed near the mountain and then continued on foot. On their way, they met a Taoist priest carrying a glass plate that held two elixirs.

The Monkey King killed him with his iron staff, and Guanyin was shocked. Wukong explained, "He is a friend of the Black Wind Monster, so he must be on his way to the monster's birthday party." Wukong lifted the body and found that it had become a wolf. He showed Guanyin the bottom of the glass plate, which was engraved with the words

Made by Taoist Lingxuzi

The Monkey King smiled, "Look at the characters engraved here. I think the Taoist's name was Lingxuzi. Transform yourself into him. I will swallow one elixir and then turn myself into a larger elixir. When you meet the monster, offer him the large elixir. Once he swallows it, I will be in his stomach. If he refuses to give the robe back, I will stir up his belly."

Things had gone so far, that Guanyin agreed to go along.

Bodhisattva Guanyin turned herself into the Taoist priest and Wukong transformed into an elixir. Before long, they arrived at the entrance to the Black Wind Monster's cave, with Guanyin holding the glass plate.

After the imp reported their arrival, the monster came to welcome her and let her in. They greeted each other and sat down.

Guanyin took the larger elixir from the plate and said, "Your Majesty, I present you with an elixir as a birthday gift. May you a live a thousand years!"

The Black Wind Monster invited Guanyin to take the other elixir while he took his. The monster opened his mouth, put the elixir in, and felt it smoothly roll down by itself.

Wukong returned to his usual form and churned wildly in the Black Wind Monster's stomach.

The monster fell to the ground, rolling in pain.

Guanyin also revealed her true appearance and asked the monster to return the robe to the Monkey King. The monster did, and Wukong flew out through the monster's nostrils.

Fearing that the monster might do evil again, Guanyin placed a hoop on his head.

The Black Wind Monster tried to jab her with his spear, but Guanyin recited the spell and the monster instantly dropped his spear in pain. He begged, "I'm ready to convert. Please spare my life."

Wukong wanted to hit the monster again but Guanyin stopped him, saying, "My sacred Luojia Mountain is unattended. I will take him back with me to be a mountain guardian."

Bodhisattva Gunayin subdued the Black Wind Monster and took him straight back to her home.

The Monkey King packed the robe safely, set it aside, and went into the Black Wind Cave. The imps inside had fled in terror. Wukong filled the cave with dry wood and set it on fire, turning it into a Red Wind Cave. Taking the robe with him, Wukong mounted a cloud and headed back to the monastery.

When Wukong did not return, Xuanzang was puzzled and wondered if his disciple had truly gone to see the Bodhisattva, or if he had just made an excuse and run away. As he wondered, a colorful mist formed in the air, and suddenly Wukong emerged from it and cried, "Master, the robe is here!"

Xuanzang was overjoyed.

The monks cheered and said, "This is wonderful! All is well! Our lives are saved."

The next morning, Wukong brushed the dragon horse and packed their luggage, and the master and his disciple continued their journey.

The monks from the monastery accompanied the two travelers for a long time, making certain they were well on their way, and bade them farewell.

Publisher's Note

All books in our The Irrepressible Monkey King series are based on the Chinese novel *Journey to the West*. Written in the 1500s during the Ming Dynasty by Wu Cheng'en, *Journey to the West* is one of the Four Great Classical Novels of Chinese literature. The story mixes myths and folklore with historical events from the 7th century. There are a few well-known translations into English, some of which are condensed, while others are complete. This book is a new translation into English from an abridged Chinese-language version of *Journey to the West*.

The original text of this work was written in Chinese. The translator, editor, and publisher have made every effort to ensure that the English-language version is as accurate as possible and in keeping with the artistic intent of the author. Because this work reflects a different culture, some of the ideas and attitudes may be unfamiliar to the English-language audience.